white

ALSO BY ROB MCLENNAN

a compact of words, 2008

Ottawa: The Unknown City, 2007

subverting the lyric: essays, 2007

The Ottawa City Project, 2007

aubade, 2006

name   , an errant, 2006

stone, book one, 2004

whats left, 2004

red earth, 2003

paper hotel, 2002

harvest, a book of signifiers, 2001

bagne, or Criteria for Heaven, 2000

The Richard Brautigan Ahhhhhhhhhhh, 1999

Manitoba highway map, 1999

bury me deep in the green wood, 1999

Notes on drowning, 1998

Missing Persons - novel in progress

white

A NOVEL BY **rob mclennan**

THE MERCURY PRESS

The publisher gratefully acknowledges the financial assistance of the Canada Council for the Arts, the Ontario Arts Council, and the Ontario Book Publishing Tax Credit Program. The publisher further acknowledges the financial support of the Government of Canada through the Department of Canadian Heritage's Book Publishing Industry Development Program (BPIDP) for our publishing activities.

Canada Council   Conseil des Arts
for the Arts   du Canada

ONTARIO ARTS COUNCIL
CONSEIL DES ARTS DE L'ONTARIO

Ontario
Ontario Media
Development
Corporation

Société de
développement
de l'industrie
des médias
de l'Ontario

Canadä

Editor: Beverley Daurio
Cover, composition and page design: Beverley Daurio
Back cover photograph of the author: Christina Riley

Printed and bound in Canada
Printed on acid-free paper

1 2 3 4 5   11 10 09 08 07

Library and Archives Canada Cataloguing in Publication

McLennan, Rob, 1970-
White / Rob Mclennan.
ISBN 978-1-55128-134-6
I. Title.
PS8575.L4586W45 2007   C813'.54   C2007-904923-0

The Mercury Press
Box 672, Station P, Toronto, Ontario Canada M5S 2Y4
www.themercurypress.ca

for miz mulligan

prologue:

□

Whoever said, a highway filled with light. A black, black lie. The greyhound bus stripped miles along dark road, through pitch-black night. The rotting smell of burning river, of forgetfulness and sorrow, and the rare passing car. Cyclops eye of lone motorcycle. Border crossings, from one world to the next, and ugly stops for no good reason. The woman who insisted on speaking to her while standing still in line, and the lies she gave in return.

Why yes, I am a student, leaving for a slight break in studies. English, she said, I'm studying English literature.

Easier to lie than to forcefully shut the old woman down, or ignore her. Even try to explain.

I'm escaping. I am going home. I am going home.

part one:

□

The day after P and H were married, P fainted in the middle of the hotel lobby beside the postcard stand. After only one night in Niagara Falls, she was unable to tell if she was revived with American or Canadian water.

She couldn't tell much of their surroundings when they arrived so late the night before, the walls paper thin for their noisemaking. P noticed it, and suggested they go for a scenic drive around the city. On whatever side they were on, she had no idea, or interest. Brown fields of tobacco, and student arms gathering crop. She suddenly felt lightheaded.

On the drive through Niagara Falls, all she could think of was Marilyn Monroe, and photographers following her around the few days she was there, young and beautiful, fragile as a hairline fracture on glass. All she thought through the view was sending a postcard to *Saturday Night* magazine, writing: I am also twenty-six, and at Niagara Falls. Please send a photographer.

□

P and H were married in a small wooden church, white steeple crouched in the woods. Filled with fire and brimstone, the larger-than-life preacher-man with arms in the air, proclaiming more than he knew, like the lead at an old-style revival meeting.

P's mother refused to go to the ceremony. She would have noth-ing to do with that man, she said, pointing her venom at H. Reflections of P's own father. What not even a mother could love, P's mother had said, a stern darkness over her face. He'll take you away from the people you love and leave you to rot, she had said. What P's father had supposedly done, marrying his young maid and moving her miles.

What P's mother had allowed to happen, never said a word, and spent years wrapped in frustration and silence. On the day P and H were married, P imagined her absent mother working the fields, col-lecting harvest. Collecting the things she had planted, since.

□

After P fainted, they spent the afternoon in their room, watching movies on pay-per-view.

There was a certain kind of absurdity about a honeymoon at Niagara Falls, P thought, but she was enjoying it. H had insisted on the Falls, although P couldn't tell why, other than the fact that H's parents had been to the same hotel on theirs, married first in Montreal and heading west. P couldn't think of any other options, any way to argue against it, so she agreed. It had happened so fast.

The way H described them, P liked to compare his parents to circus performers, if only in her head. They would have gone to Las Vegas to get married in an Elvis chapel, if they'd had their way. If only Nevada were closer.

H likes to pretend that his parents are dry, boring and non-ironic. P isn't sure if it's because he disapproves of the joke, or simply doesn't get it. She has been afraid to ask.

□

P remembered a garden, a back yard open space, but she didn't remember where she slept the night before.

□

From the newspaper the previous week, a clipping P had saved of a Chinese girl and her American boyfriend who killed her parents, because her father didn't approve of the young couple dating. It seemed an extreme way to solve a problem, but P wanted to exclude no options. Just see her way clear. She decided instead not to answer the phone, but H accused her of being passive-aggressive.

History is written by those who make it, or the victors; she can never quite remember. Years from now, she thinks, she will tell her children about the second man she ever loved; about how her mother didn't approve but she went ahead and married him anyway. About the house they lived in, deep in the suburbs, and the breaking of eventual lines. If she ever does have children. And what if the children were also his? To even think such things seems a betrayal. She closes her eyes, leaves her body in the beige kitchen and lets the room fade to black. There are Christmas decorations on the inside of her head. They feel dark; coloured lights flickering deep red, dark blue, heavy green.

☐

Sometimes at night, dreaming, H twitches his body against P's in his sleep. H's body always feels cold to her. He won't tell her what he dreams about. P suspects that he dreams about work. Other times, P wonders if H has nightmares so horrible that H is afraid to tell her any of them. If H remembers them at all.

□

One day, a stray dog wanders onto their street. P spends the whole morning coaxing it into the house with promises and teasings of food. It's a big dog, with thick black scraggly hair, and is wary of strangers, and P's advances. When it finally nears, and enters the house, P closes the door. The dog panics, and spends half an hour running in circles, looking for a way out, knocking over tables and plants, before it calms down and eats the food that P offers. Drinks from the cereal bowl from the floral-print set P's mother had mailed as a wedding gift.

Eventually lets P get close, but not too close, a trust in borders and boundaries. P hopes that H will love the dog as she does. She has already given it a name — Cerberus. The protector of the underworld.

When H gets home from work, he yells at P for bringing in such a scruffy animal, and chases it out the back door with a broomstick. P locks herself in the bedroom and doesn't talk to H for two days.

□

When P was a little girl, her father would come into her room to tuck her in, and tell her about the ghost in the house, there for over a hundred years, that protected her as she slept. To keep P from jumping at shadows and vague noises, the century-old house shifting.

P in her large house with H, she knows: there is no protection here.

□

P dreams regularly of roses. Bright red bursts in bushes full and green, by the entrance to a cave. The roses are thick, and red like clotting blood. There is a darkness in the cave just as thick, to the point of flammability. Every morning, with the sun, the roses swell to bursting, and open like small, fresh wounds. By the evening, a gust of wind rushes forth from the cave, and causes the flowers to wilt, and decay, as though the life had been torn from them. Petals wither and brown, and collapse to the ground.

This is a familiar dream, hidden somewhere behind P's memory, a dream P has had before.

□

One day she tells H, you are the second man I have ever loved. H is watching television. He doesn't ask about the first. Which is good, because P can't remember. She doesn't even remember where her photo albums are, packed away in boxes somewhere; her mother's house, maybe. Pictures would help her remember. P's mother won't bring them over, and H hasn't gone to get them. He keeps saying, later, later. P never learned how to drive. Why, when there was always her mother to take her places she needed to go, or boys willing to pull up the driveway in their fast cars, one after another, to take her on a night out? She doesn't know where any of these boys have disappeared to, ten years later. Other girls in other houses, other laneways, other nights on the town, behind the drive-in theatre. None of them have aged in her remembering.

□

One day, P decides to write a children's story, about The Little Shortbread Man, after the cookies her mother used to make. But, because shortbread is soft, and the little man still fresh and warm, his left leg breaks off twenty paces into his escapist sprint, and the village predators pounce on his fresh-baked flesh, devouring him: woodcutter, old woman, and the like. It sounds like a story from her childhood. P abandons her story. She wonders what H would have thought.

□

P finds it strange living in a house with no past.

Before their marriage, H had been living here for some time, but the house looks barren to the point of abandoned. H finds it comforting; no baggage. That they can start from a beginning and so doing, move forward.

Everything should have a history, P says. It gives you a place from which to move.

H is blind to such things. He doesn't understand the apprehension of starting a new life with cupboards bare, and drawers empty but for a few take-out and delivery fliers she's been collecting, left in the mailbox. There has to be a history. H doesn't understand her need for clutter.

Sometimes P goes outside to smell the dirt in their makeshift garden, that she carved out of their backyard, to be planted in spring. What there is of a yard, barely big enough to contain a small car. P talks about planting geraniums in the spring. She talks about planting forget-me-nots. She orders things out of the seed catalogue when H is at work, and accumulates supplies for the end of six months, even though it's barely fall.

□

A week after they were married, H discovered a potato partially blocking the tailpipe of his car. What had been making P feel sick and dizzy — carbon monoxide — somehow hadn't affected him. It must have been there since the ceremony, H suggested, based on how P had been feeling. She suspected her mother, but didn't want to say anything until she knew for sure. Or even if she did.

□

Living in the suburbs for the first time, P begins to see how people live. Where houses fit together like Nordic brick, visions of Lego blocks, row on identical row. Here, the standards still apply: men go off in the morning with briefcases, sometimes before the sun, leaving women and small children to their own devices. In some houses, both husband and wife leave, and children are given to caregivers, grandparents, daycare. Wherever it is small children go.

P wants to be one of those women, desperately. She wants to have somewhere to go.

But she knows, too, that this is where serial killers originate, and child molesters. Where teenagers group, gang and swarm, for no other reasons than boredom. Middle-aged men with caches of computer porn involving animals, children. She knows this, that it is true. P has read the statistics, the newspapers, seen the talk shows. She will not leave the house today. She will not leave the house.

□

The day P and H were married, P's mother took the harvest in.
Corn stalks withered to brown.

□

P starts to go through H's collection of boxes in the basement, and finds an old Latin textbook. She begins to leave notes for him around the house in fractured Latin — "buy more toilet paper," or "clean the fridge" — wondering how much he might remember from his classes.

After a few weeks with no response, H is cornered. He admits to P that he never took Latin in university, but a roommate of his had, and H hadn't got around to selling or throwing out any of the books when he moved.

□

P thinks that H has the biggest eyes she's ever seen. She knows the story, how a girl is supposed to fall for the man most like her father. P draws a blank; her mother destroyed all the pictures of her father years ago. White spaces in their photo albums. When P's father died, her mother took an exacto-knife to them, like a scalpel, carving out bits of her own life; her history. As though P never had a father; as though P's mother had formed her from the soil and grown her from a single seed produced from her body.

Whenever H is inside her, moving on top of her white body, P wants to reach up with her tongue, and put it on one of H's eyes. To discover how they taste.

□

H told P that the first thing he noticed about P was the way that she smelled, even before he saw her. Of open spaces, fields of wild-flowers, and shortbread. The two of them in a pub at the edge of the same water, she travelled from one direction, and he from the other. Vacationing, they told each other, at the same time, in the same sea-side town. She wore a yellow sundress, and had sparkles in her eyes.

After various small talk, they walked through the market and shared a pomegranate. P flirted recklessly; threatened with a sly smile to eat ice cream with her feet, but his eyes wore her down, calmed her.

In those initial moments, P didn't trust H because he wouldn't smile. He still doesn't smile, P thinks, but he sometimes laughs.

□

When asked, P has always sidestepped the issue of family history. Sometimes she remembers that her mother is dead, and other times she remembers that she's not.

□

H and P in their antiseptic house at the end of a road that has yet to exist. The smell of fresh-cut wood and wet gravel, anticipating pavement; wave upon wave of new construction flooding the woods and the plain. Their two bedroom bath, sunken divide into living room floor from the space beneath chandelier, where the dining room table would sit, planted new from IKEA.

P waits a whole day for delivery, pacing the hardwood and finally arriving at the door the same time H does from work, the dog at the gate not knowing which of the two to turn on, first; restless at the threshold.

Lego and IKEA, P thinks; why are her suburban metaphors European?

□

To prepare for Hallowe'en, P spends most of two weeks decorating the house with bits of string and scraps of coloured paper, spotting the walls and hanging them from the ceiling. She found a store that had images left from Thanksgiving, the horn of plenty and other paraphernalia that she tapes to windows and the front door, and non-committal collages of paper in strange shapes.

When children arrive at the front door, adorned with ghost and witch costumes, bright and dark colours under warm coats for the candy that H brought home, P won't let any of them in. She refuses to answer the door.

□

P has a hard time remembering what her father looked like. He died when she was six, and she can remember things he said, and events that involved the two of them, but his face remains a mystery.

When P was seventeen, she compared a photograph of her mother to her own face in the bathroom mirror, searching out the differences. Those, she decided, would be the parts that belonged to her father. She struggled to form an image.

□

P and H met and were married in the space of a week. Neither of them was known for an impulsive nature; at least, that's what they each had told the other.

It was electric, sharing exotic fruit on the beach. H's fingers easing fleshy bits of pomegranate into P's mouth. Even though, P said to herself, it made no sense.

It didn't seem to matter that neither of them knew any details about the other. H said that he worked in computers, building networks. P said that her parents were dead.

□

One day, the dog returns, more eager for P's affections and attentions. Lets P brush its coat, remove most of the clumps of hair and matted dirt. How thin the dog's body is.

When H gets home, P stands her ground. The dog stays. H relents, but the dog keeps its wary eye on him. It still won't let either of them stand behind, where the dog can't see. P decides that the dog is a him. With its thick hair, and until they can get close enough, it's impossible to tell.

And the dog's movements are slow and cautious; it even pees outside where they can't see; withdrawn, so they might never know.

□

P can no longer remember the face of the first man she ever loved. They were barely teenagers, and spent two weeks living on the grounds of Expo '86, after the world's fair had ended. P's heart had raced with anticipation. A brush of his hand.

He had only to look. Flowers bloomed where he walked. They spent two explosive weeks hiding behind new buildings and the remains of entertainments, before it was over. A bomb dropped in her mother's living room. And now, P can't remember his name, or what he looked like. The colour of his hair.

□

Lately, P has started watching daytime television. Talk shows on cooking, clothes and violence, and women who love too much; convicts who marry their victims. Country singers tearing Christmas carols to shreds.

Every day on the news, there is someone killing someone else with a weapon, and endless variations. She has started keeping a log. A woman who kills her sleeping husband with an axe, for his infidelity. The boy, too young to be prosecuted, who shoots and kills an elderly neighbour. The man who caves in the heads of wife and children with a hammer. Crushing blows to the skull, and bodies found in remote woods.

□

P finds it strange that there are no photos of H anywhere among his possessions. On one shelf, an envelope of crumbling brown and white, black and white, of children he says are his parents and others — uncles, aunts, grandparents.

□

The only books P can find on H's shelf that interest her: the tale of Orpheus, the myth of Odysseus, Dante's *Inferno*, the *Gideon New Testament*.

□

Sometimes in the mornings, P goes for walks in their neighbourhood, but doesn't tell H. H encourages P to stay near the house. In the first month they lived together, P went out to explore on foot, and after a few hours, couldn't find her way home. She spent much of the day wandering in circles, streets with names that were nearly hers but not, with hundreds of identical houses, yards, small parks. By late afternoon, she found a gas station and had to call H at work to come find her. When he got there, she was standing by the blue phone booth, defeated and deflated, eyes red from crying, a fifteen-minute walk from home.

□

One day, a woman from the nearby collection of houses invites P to a Tupperware party, so she can be introduced to, and make friends with, the neighbours. Other women who live there.

P is wary of the women who live around her, and thinks that the one at her front door looks haggard, old. P realizes that she is probably the same age, but P doesn't have the weight of small children hanging off her limbs during the day, like jewellery, or overripe fruit.

P tells the woman very calmly that she has enough friends, which is an obvious lie, thank you very much, and closes the door. The woman with the bad haircut stands for a moment on the doorstep, then leaves.

P has no interest in parties, Tupperware or otherwise. She has enough containers, and containers are only good if you have things to put in them.

□

From the front window, P watches the snow cover everything. Parking spaces, kids' bicycles, the front walk. P feels the misery of things to come. P is getting used to being alone.

□

One day, P dares to go out and discovers a strip mall near the house, a small row of stores including video rental, a bank, and about half a dozen others. Only a twenty-minute walk. She sees a flower shop, and goes in, letting the smells of green and pollen overwhelm her.

P spends a long time looking through the flowers and small trees, lets the fragrances fill her breath.

P sees that they are hiring, and takes an application form home to fill out, without telling H.

□

P is in the house when winter comes, and stays. It snows for three full days and shuts down airports throughout the eastern seaboard, packing blue and white six feet high at both doors. H clears a path when he gets home, with a shovel he keeps in the car.

P has the heat turned on high, as much as it can go, but still she feels cold. She shudders up against one of the heat vents in the front room. The dog refuses to leave her side.

No matter what's happening on the outside, H says, it feels like a sauna in the house. Finally opening the front door, he says, it feels like spring.

□

P finds a newspaper article about the body of an elderly woman
found in a snowbank, half a block from the apartment building where
she lived. The police and neighbours had realized how she fell and was
unable to pull herself free from the deep snow. In the middle of the
day on a busy street, no one noticed. Three days later, her frozen body
found deep under since-ploughed snow.

Such things strengthen P's resolve not to venture forth from the
front steps. The onslaught of snow, and her new husband, rendered
invisible. She dreams of white crocuses; she dreams of bluebells. In the
pit of her stomach, P feels the pain of something but can't quite place
it. A kind of loss, perhaps. A kind of emptiness.

□

On the day P met H, she was thinking of flowers. The daughter of a gardener, one who worked and knew the earth, she had memorized the names of trees and wildflowers. Running the list through her head when H appeared — roses, crocuses, violets, irises, hyacinths, narcissi.

What the earth grew as an enchanting lure. The colour of his eyes and the way that he looked at her. A hundred hearts and a fragrance that pleased the sky, the earth, and the sea. What went beyond the scope of her will.

What P saw in his eyes: a hundred other eyes, and in those too, each a hundred more, turning back from green, from blue, from grey.

She admits to becoming lost. She admits to stepping off the clean sharp edge of earth.

□

P remembers a garden, and wonders if the garden remembers her.

Rummaging around the basement, P finds an unopened box of books in a corner, fifteen years worth of collections of Doonesbury comic strips. She spends days reading them, without knowing previously of half the events being described, being young when they happened.

P remembers a garden, and she remembers her mother.

In a dream, D tends her garden, watching the buds rise on green stalks, the small movements making themselves large, and ripening. She tends her garden. D realizes that this is a dream. Everything browns to dust.

D wakes up miles away, in another part of the same country.

□

Very quietly, H takes up smoking. To ease, he says, the stress at work, although if challenged, he'd be hard pressed to explain exactly what those stresses are. He stands his days outside his building; alone in a small crowd, inhaling cold air and filtered tobacco.

P can smell it on his clothes when he gets home. The antiseptic smell of the new house makes H radiate smoke like a stench when he takes off his coat. H presumes that no one can tell; P can taste it in his mouth, and through the pores of his skin.

About the same time, P does laundry more often, but H doesn't make the connection. The hamper in their bedroom never gets more than half-full. Or, as a pessimist might say, half-empty.

□

Within a matter of days of moving in, P realized, there was nothing around where they lived but houses, schools, parks. Nothing for her to do, or see. No entertainments. The buses ran every half hour or hour, depending, and never according to schedule. The neighbourhood children ran across the front walk, stealing the ornaments and the barbecue.

There were people everywhere, out on lawnchairs on the weekend drinking beer straight from bottles, and talking loudly. During the day, P couldn't step out either door without having to acknowledge someone she had no interest in talking to; someone who lived like her.

□

P reads books about past-life regression and reincarnation. H says he doesn't believe her, and taunts her about reincarnation, and the lonely hopes of connecting to famous dead people.

What if you discover that you're the reincarnation of some bored nineteen-fifties housewife, he asks, or a nineteenth-century London prostitute?

That would never happen, P says. She doesn't consider it a valid argument. She's only interested in lives that made a difference. That's what's important.

H accuses P of being elitist, and arrogant. P says that H is being deliberately cruel. P considers swallowing all the pills from the bathroom cabinet until she remembers that they don't have any. They don't have a storehouse going back years; various coloured pills in plastic vials her mother hadn't thrown out yet, some going back to when she was little. Her father's heart medicine.

If you believe in reincarnation at all, H ends, you have to allow for unmemorable lives. Every action defines character, he says, and then goes back into the basement to his trains.

□

On the weekends, H spends his time in the basement, working on model trains. There is an absence of locked rooms in the house. P wonders if he has ever heard of Bluebeard.

H talks about putting a bar in the basement, fully stocked, of course. When would he even have time to use it, P wonders. Where would he find space to put it, with his trains in the way. After months of their marriage, she still hasn't met any of H's co-workers, so doesn't know if the appearance of a bar in their basement would be a negative or positive thing. They would have to start calling it the rec room instead of the basement. Where you do your laundry, and keep empty boxes. The naming of certain things dependent only on how they are used.

P's parents had one, once, called the playroom, where she would build cities out of Lego blocks, caves from blankets and pillows, and armies on the moon. Create flower paths from construction paper patterns. Cut out a circle for sun.

□

When P was young, her mother read poems to her, as P's grand-father had done to D. Not just the classics, but modern as well. D used to say of her father, if he didn't learn a new poem by memory once a month, he felt strangely guilty. Poems by Keats, and Thomas' *A Child's Christmas in Wales*. Fragments of "The Wasteland."

She was the only child in grade three who knew "The Improved Binoculars" by heart.

As P was growing up, she had imagined herself as a character in a Gwendolyn MacEwen poem. Alive, and filled with magic.

□

In P's mind, women are the keepers of memory, although she feels as though she has none.

□

Before she was engaged, P recalls living in an apartment downtown. One bedroom, and all the space she needed.

She lived above a convenience store and a pub, and knew the names of the staff. She had spent a few summers waitressing, keeping herself entertained through a series of regular customers.

The blind senior every weekday at one, who drank coffee and told bad jokes, flirting harmlessly before leaving alone in his cab home. The businessmen who came in singularly or in small groups, for lunch, pitchers of beer and the newspapers.

It was the summer she gained new appreciation for classic rock — Steely Dan, The Moody Blues, The Five Man Electrical Band.

□

As soon as P and H returned from their honeymoon to the recently constructed house, boxes of her possessions waiting for them, H left her to go off to work in the morning, and left her. Many of his things were already unpacked; had been for some time.

P left her belongings in boxes, half wondering if her mother would come by and remove her at gunpoint. D had always warned P of the evils of living with a man, especially one she was married to.

Even though she didn't believe in D's warnings, P was compelled by them, for reasons she didn't even notice. Like carrying a substantial bruise on your thigh, without even realizing you'd been hurt.

□

H and P's mother had decided to hate each other. P isn't sure where it began, but she knows where it is now. Like a river, not always sure where it started, miles beyond the fields, but sure of the part that tore through the house.

P's mother only calls when H is at work. It's the only time that she would. It's the only time H allows.

□

One night, P has a dream that she is a pre-industrial Madam in a small American town, an abandoned winery hidden beneath the house, with the entrance behind the fireplace. Everything is dark, black or brown, and the air tastes like cinnamon.

Somewhere in the dream, an ambitious and villainous man finds out about her inactive winery, and tries to purchase it. The spirits of dead workers killed in the accident that closed the winery down, who live in the unused space, are against the sale.

In her grief at being discovered, she goes to one of the dead men and holds him; calling him better than Dorian Gray, he who will never age.

H's alarm goes off, and P is shaken briefly from her reverie. She breaks completely when the snooze alarm goes off nine minutes later.

□

One morning, after H leaves for work, P notices the snow finally beginning to melt. White turned to brown, slipping slowly away.

part two:

□

During the day, in the third week of April, H returned home from work, and P was gone. H had no idea where. He couldn't even speculate.

H had long wondered what she did during the day, if there could have been a clue there, but P had just as long deflected him. She was always there when he arrived home. The big black monster of a dog giving the evil eye.

Phone calls home to see how she was were pointless. She refused to answer even when the two were home.

But this, the last snow gone and so was she. The house, that had barely contained them, was empty of her things.

What he thought the strangest part, their small backyard, torn up by trowel, bare dirt naked among the green scraps. Not a corner had been spared. As though she were preparing to find something, or bury it.

□

After the first twenty-four hours of P's disappearance, H visited the police. To H, the police were polite but useless; to the police, H was barely that. No trace, no note, no suggestion, but not gone long enough to be a worry on their end. They spoke vacation, family. Affairs?

H didn't like the suggestion.

It's more romantic this way, she said, when he would ask about the suitcase always packed, under the bed, and she would distract him with a touch. The slight rise of her short skirt.

Married nearly a year, and yet you've never met any of her family, the police asked. Puzzled.

For some reason, H had a memory of a mother living in northern Ontario. Bobcaygeon?

Love can do strange things, but H began to wonder. They offered him little solace; a phone number, and a suggestion of hospitals, morgues.

H left the police station feeling weak, empty.

◻

H didn't sleep much the first night. He slept even less, the second.

There is such a thing, he realized, as being invisible.

Pain is an object that can be held as well as dropped, as easily and as difficult as letting go. Pain can be harvested.

□

What happens when you are abandoned. Small seeds scattered throughout the house. It was a question his young wife had asked more than once.

But what did H know. Please help me, she'd ask, but he had no idea how, or even what was happening to her.

Small moments, here and there. Afraid to take root. That she would be fine for stretches, and then. Crawling around on the floor so she couldn't be seen by neighbours. For a matter of weeks, a couple of shots of tequila first thing in the morning. Because, she said, she didn't like breakfast cereal. A small collapse of the arteries. The ongoing snow and cold, a whole winter cabin still, indoors, threatening to engulf her. It was as though she had succumbed to a fever, huddling against the chill.

What happens when you are abandoned. When you know you have been abandoned. The loss well before she actually left.

Heartbreaks on the floor and moving like a machine. He pulled a cigarette from his pack, out of habit more than anything else. What did it matter. The lighter switch. Another glass of whiskey.

□

H felt nothing. He found it hard to occupy this new absence. The house as it stood, barely but bare. The presence that was hers, seeing how it filled the empty corners.

The dog, too. She must have taken it. One relief.

H thought a long time about what he didn't know about P. About their beginnings, and hurried wedding, telling no one until they made their way home. Caught up in carefree bliss.

What do you do when your wife is gone. You find her. When she has disappeared. What do you do?

H spent a week's worth of evenings in a crowded pub, close to the house.

part three:

□

When P first arrived home on her mother's doorstep, her mother stared until she regained breath. Not a word. Back to doing dishes; as though five years had not opened such a silence between them.

P poured herself a drink from the fridge, and sat down at the kitchen table.

A lot can happen in five years. D could see from her face, this was no longer the young girl who had left. Her face looked worn, and tired, yet relieved, as though a weight had been lifted.

Her one bag on the floor, and no evidence of car; bus on the highway, or a hitchhike from town, it didn't matter how she got there.

P went upstairs to her old room, unchanged in the time, and slept. The sleep of someone returned, seeking direction, comfort. She slept for two full days, to the point that at times she appeared almost dead; didn't stir when her mother appeared and disappeared with meals left on the bedside, hot to eventual cold.

□

In her dreams, P, with three childhood friends at the seashore, picks flowers. Watches the water roll, thick and as restless as reeds.

Very suddenly it grows dark; the four girls gasp and drop their pickings. Clouds avail themselves of black, and water rises sharp as blades.

The girls work for cover, but the shelter around is thin and distant. The air blackens to oil and moves in. Overcomes.

P wakes to finger-taps on window and the air-conditioner. Rain. Only rain.

□

P presented D with a weakness, a chink in her finely worked armour. When she was P's age, raising her own child alone and abandoned, kicking against anything or anyone who got in the way. Made of sterner stuff.

D left home when she was fifteen. Ran away, after her father's near-misses had begun to connect. When she threatened it, her mother had helped pack.

To this day, unsure if her mother's help was a ploy, a trick. For D to relent; to see what she would do next.

Two years in the city, she waitressed in a Greek restaurant, lying about her age to work. Between busy stretches, and verbal abuse from the owner, D pushed her change into the jukebox, for songs she used to know. Songs that would give her pause; make her think before she spoke. Well up in her dark eyes and collect there. As Stavros, the owner, would yell in her direction, whyfor you spend all your money to cry?

□

P's memory as selective as her wardrobe, like a switch turned to the opposite position. Five years near erased, or stored in some other, unused location.

□

Every Wednesday, the county newspaper places her. The weekly two-sectioned print that reminds her where she has come. Or has returned to.

Photographs of old friends, and the children of old friends. The park with the outdoor stage she remembers, and the boy who once took her there, after a while. The stage is long gone, and replaced. Even in her memory, nothing remains the same.

The week she goes into town with her mother, P can repeat back the history of every building on Main Street, one hundred years back or more. Where the shoe store once was, the general store with the creaking wood floors and the rain barrel, or the law office that once held the library, below the apartment where her mother's great-uncle used to live.

P has to close her eyes eventually; gets a headache just from look-ing at the storefronts. The entire history of a single speck comes down on her full force. She begins to cry. The absence of history weighs heavy.

□

P stirs sugar into her coffee, and wonders what the fates have in store for her. The ladies. Awash in the damp and slightly rotting smell she associated with her mother, and her mother's strong hands. An imprint left on P's shoulders before her mother went outside to work. Mixed with the smell of bread still warm from the previous night's oven, cooling on the kitchen counter.

Now that she's here, in her mother's house, in what was once her house, where she was meant to be, what is P to do with herself? The question asked itself. She stirs her coffee and she listens to her mother outside starting the tractor. The smell of her hands comes in through the window; her mother with the plow making streaks in the yard.

The question asks itself.

□

During her days on her mother's couch, P thinks about home, and what exactly that means. The shifts between where she was then and where she is now. How the house is so much smaller now, almost confining.

P remembers whole mornings lying under the living-room table reading crime novels, and she wonders how it is she fit; resting chin on her arms staring out her bedroom window. She remembers the curtains of rain coming in during storms, and pulling away everything beyond her boundaries of land and flesh, removing everything beyond her, that was somehow not real.

P stares out her window, crouched down to mimic her former view. There are no former views, only echoes. Memories behind her eyes, that overlap and confuse against what she sees out there. Even though she can't see them, P now knows the names of the towns that exist over the horizon, and the names of the cities beyond.

P feels the fates working against her. The ache of age and the time past.

So much of her life she worked hard to reject, but rushed back on her, twisting intestines.

P has grown weary of feeling. P has grown weary, even old.

□

P plants the tulip bulbs in a corner of her mother's garden, the ones she arrived with. Her mother all day in her greenhouse, planting twigs.

P's mother teaches at the agricultural college an hour's drive back. P was six years old when her mother got the position, at work just enough to keep her house and home, and home long enough to sustain what she had. There was no square foot of land on the two hundred acres that her mother hadn't dug with her hands, to plant, pull, or to save. Or to bury. The sticks and the stones still up against the back forty for pets P no longer knew the names of, and other pets since, her mother would forget.

□

There is the cigarette, and then there is the dream of the cigarette.

□

The photo albums; books that had not been moved over the time she was away. Books that had been added. P ran her fingers along the spines of the familiar and the not-so-familiar on her mother's shelf. The volumes of history and naming, adrift between what was there, and, no longer.

P and her fingers on the spines played piano keys, rolling water forth and back, a harp of many-coloured strings. She stopped at random, pulling at the neck a photo-album spine to crack open; to see what she would see. To see what she could remember.

□

A morning, D in her apron, baking bread. Pounding loaves between classes, the dog in the corner, eyes in the back of its head. It twitches and lifts as P moves noiseless down stairs.

On the hall bookshelf, P finds the detritus of another journal, the last that she kept before leaving; bad poetry, and long-winded complaints. A dream of rose bushes.

□

From her mother's training, P can still identify the flowers simply by their seeds: hydrangea, orchid, tulip, rose. An immunity to other skills, but a knowledge she so steadily maintains. Steady in her days, she returns to the garden and her mother's hands, hands that were soft, to never see a scar, no matter the scratch. The hardened palm and the open fist.

When P was a girl, she had always asked her mother for a pet, but D would never allow it; I refuse, she would say, to let a cat or a dog run roughshod through the house, or dig up rosebushes to deposit their leavings. Spiral notebooks from pre-adolescence; she'd carved in sketches of cats and dogs in the dozens from her elementary years, giving shapes and names to their absence. Giving them colours, personalities, voice. Virtual pets she knew only by ink, and by touch.

Always draw the blade away when you cut, her mother said, never toward.

These are but a few of the things her mother taught; that her mother had left her.

□

P was pregnant. It was as much a shock to her as anyone. The doctor with the snapping gloves confirmed it. She didn't like the way he looked; she didn't like his leering smile, or the way he tried to talk down to soothe her. As though she were a child who'd done something wrong, unsavoury. She didn't like his eyebrows, burly grey and pointing up at the ends, making him appear Satanic.

She hated him for confirming it, and held her loathing on the surface of her skin. Goosebumps. This thing she hadn't even suspected, despite the bad mornings she'd had, and lightheadedness, the cramps. This wriggling foreign thing inside her body, growing, an uninvited guest.

It must have happened when she was sleeping. Some crawling thing or evil beast had entered her, and laid eggs. An egg.

Death, she thought. I will call the baby Death, for that is how I feel: dying, slow.

Removal didn't occur to her. Not once.

D squeezed her hand. P startled, jumped. She had forgotten her mother was there.

□

D pulls weeds from her garden one by one. Beige gloves and a wide-brimmed hat. Her old-lady hat, she calls it. D preferred not to use sprays or poisons on her crops, instead methodically going over everything by hand. Years earlier, D remembers, a couple down the road had given birth to a baby so badly deformed, that once born, breathed only minutes before the lungs collapsed.

Not even developed enough to have chosen a gender, the name-less infant hermaphrodite gasping, turned blue. D felt ill thinking about it. Why did she feel ill. She pushed inside the kitchen door past P, and was sick in the sink.

□

P remembers a garden, and wonders if the garden remembers her.

At the back of her mother's lot, P stands and stares at open fields. The rustle of corn a whisper; the wind through the wheat a meandered hush.

The insects tore at her through the walk out, and P slapped at her own flesh to fight them off.

It was as though she was being eaten alive, consumed by the place itself. It felt like drowning, consumed by the very waves.

□

D wonders out loud what P expects to do, pushing quietly, soft. In the whole of her life, P is the only person D doesn't know how to deal with, confront head on. D has no patience for tiptoeing, such nonsense.

P sits on the couch peeling oranges, popping wedges into her mouth in front of the television; the small pulse of her belly edging slowly out. The evidence of baby made visible.

P counts her life out in days, even as her mother counts weeks; weeks, as opposed to seasons, paying more attention to the baby doctor than did her own wayward daughter. It's as though her daughter spends entire days half asleep, or floating underwater, far away from the concerns of the world inside her, or around.

□

As P remembers, the years of her mother and her god-awful hat, horrified she would ever leave the house, wandering the garden under a gaudy, expansive brim. Her mother would only laugh; not that there was anyone to see.

□

Picking organic from her mother's low shelf, Virginia Woolf and *The Waves*.

P knows, when you drop a book in the bath, you're supposed to immediately slip it sopping wet in the freezer, so the pages don't warp. Everybody knows that.

When it finally happens, she isn't quite sure how much time is allowed between drop and save, or save and freeze. P steps out of her mother's tub quick as silver, fishing the volume, and forgoes the towel, padding bare feet down carpeted stairs, and into the kitchen, dripping wet and naked.

Standing in her mother's kitchen, water a breadcrumb trail back, P feels a sense of divine accomplishment; a freezer-door breath, she feels sudden on skin what she's done, and burns red, full in the face and more.

□

Even as a child, P knew dirt was good for digestion.

She crawls through her mother's garden, ripping weeds from the ground with gloved hands not her own, fully aware of the bulge beneath her, like an egg, swirling above her pelvis; the gravity of her nether realms brushing turned earth.

P pauses, picks up a small clump of dirt the size of a marble, and plucks it into her mouth like a grape, swallowing it whole.

□

P stares down at her bulging mid-section. The round shape of vowel slowly rising. Or lower-case constant.

The kicking squirming thing inside that had recently caused her operatic vowels between sleep. Low, moaning sounds strung like pearls on the upstairs carpet, or sharp, staccato nails, thrust deep in the walls of her old bedroom.

To steady herself, she breathed, and moved her eyes from poster to fading poster in the soft summer dark, composing a list in her head of where her former idols were now — drug overdose, suicide, jail, security guard. Their twelve labours, that could no longer redeem them.

Her long, fallen heroes.

□

On her mother's television, P follows the story of a local girl in her late twenties, gone missing on her bicycle, on one of the nature trails.

Every day provides a further lack of new information; a fruitless search providing nothing. Equal hope, and hopelessness.

A week later, the police find the woman's body in the river, bare miles down from where they had her twelve-speed, days before.

P is distraught. The girl was barely older than she is. People aren't supposed to die on television, she thinks; and not this close to her.

People aren't supposed to die at all.

□

P searches her closet for her photo albums, but they're gone. Years of past lives. She's gone through all the boxes in her closet, under her bed, the clothes in the dresser drawers. The day as a whole feels hollow, and the ache in her chest rings endless through her rib cage.

You took them when you left, her mother says, facing the sink, drying hands on a tea towel.

□

P does not understand how this thing inside her had arrived at all. What would surely kill her in the end.

A gift from the deathless gods, no doubt, or a punishment; a condition of divine will. Appearing parthenogenetically, without benefit of male.

□

P had always felt some part of her a blank slate, to be painted upon. Painted over, if it did not suit.

When she abandoned him, the first man she ever loved at the shore, or when he abandoned her. Stephen, his name was Stephen. So sure, young and in love, leaving her home and she knew, to recreate herself, at his mere gesture. To make herself new, as some strong, adventuring woman. So much in love, with him and his promises, and that they could just drive drive drive until there was nothing left but the sun.

She was Helen, as the armies marched on, and the fields behind burned. She was Cleopatra, saved by her Caesar. She was Bonnie to his Clyde, dodging bullets as they drove. She was something feral, something strong. I want and I want, she said, and I also want.

But never Icarus; she felt more like Icarus' father, who knew not to get too close. P knew. She was the one who lived.

□

Her days a series of broken limbs, P feels weightless on her mother's couch. Her figure, grown, holds her fixed to the spot.

Every so often, to regain feeling to tingling extremities, she lifts her arms and her legs and lets herself float, falling leaf to the cold autumn ground.

P's cravings have become more, and more often. Various confections, fruits and frozen-dessert flavours. Pickles, sorbets and seasonal berries, all of which D is beholden to provide, and simply appear with, in hand.

Whenever D would start in on her gentle prodding of P's silence, and whereabouts, or even the nature of the father, P held firm in her deflection.

In her head, D compared it to an extended version of John Lennon's "lost weekend," the eighteen months he spent away from Yoko. It was best avoided, and forgotten, according to P's stares. It would not be discussed.

□

In all her life, P had never had a credit card, a bank account, or a phone in her name. It was as though her life could not be found on any map.

P remembered nothing of the intervening years, away from her mother, acting as though they had never happened. For all she knew, she might have walked into a house occupied by another family, instead of her own.

□

Patricia, her mother said softly in her sleepy ear, and put a hand to her long hair. She remembered that name, and some of the things that went with it. The boy in the bubble and the sound of her father's voice. The list of plant rotations in the backyard, and her hands in warm soil, up to the elbows when she was five.

That girl that she was, is. Does she even recall, and what comes flooding in.

☐

In her sleep, P could still feel the pomegranate seed, there in her mouth. Lodged, in the space of a lost filling. She could feel it with her tongue, but could not remove it.

In her sleep she knew; H was coming for her.

Thanks to the usual suspects: Stephen Cain, for giving it a once-over; various other ears and eyes for conversation and company, quiet and loud. Thanks to Sean + Kira + Neil + Thea at the ottawa international writers festival for simply *being*, and being so supportive. Thanks to Ann-Marie and Kate and Jennifer and Stephen and Monty and Gwendolyn who have kept me alive, often despite myself. Thanks to Bev Daurio for thoughtful eye and pen, and everyone else at The Mercury Press for doing what they do.

MARQUIS

Marquis Book Printing Inc.

Québec, Canada
2007